We were gonna have a baby, but

We had an angel instead

by Pat Schwiebert
illustrated by Taylor Bills

Grief Watch
Portland, Oregon

D1401072

We were gonna have a baby, but we had an angel instead.

My mommy had a **baby** in her tummy.

I was real excited about that most of the time.

I thought about playing ball with my baby,

And building a fort,

and playing tricks on our parents.

I loved to listen to the baby,

and talk to the baby,

and I really liked it when the baby would knock
on Mommy's tummy to get my attention.

But something happened.   The Baby died.

Our baby is not going to live with us.

We are all sad right now.

Mommy sits in the rocking chair, holding the baby's blanket
and cries a lot.

Daddy is building a box to put some of the
baby's presents in.

Even Grandy and Pops wish the baby would have stayed.

I'm sad too, but I think they are sadder.

Grandy says
the baby
can always live
in our
hearts.

People send us flowers and cards, but we still miss our baby.

If this just happened to you, I'm sorry you got an angel
instead of a baby.

I think having a baby would have been more fun.

How to help your children

Even as you grieve because of the death of your baby, you will also need to help your other children confront and manage their own grief over the loss of a sibling. Reading this book with your other children can be one way of beginning this process. We offer the following additional suggestions to help you to help them.

Children are not miniature adults. Your children will not grieve in quite the same way that you will grieve. For example:

Children are less likely to experience continual and intense grief reactions. It is not unusual to see children acting out grief one minute and then playing happily the next minute. This does not mean they are "over it". Children's minds seem to have a way of protecting them from what is too powerful to handle all at once.

On the other hand, the overall process of active grieving may last longer for a child than for an adult. As children mature they will ask more sophisticated questions about the baby who died and put that new information into their growing understanding of death.

Small children are not capable of abstract thinking and so will respond with directness to what they experience. They are looking for facts to help them understand death. At the same time, children's questions and fears are not always put into words. They will tend to act out their anger, fears, denial, wishful thinking and other manifestations of grief. Watching your children at play will give you good clues about how they are dealing with the loss.

Children are repetitive in their grief. They may ask the same questions over and over, sometimes because they want a different answer and sometimes because they just don't understand. Children's repeated questions are their attempts to take in the meaning of the family's loss.

Children grieve as part of a family, and they want to feel included in the family's experience of loss. Even with very small children it does no good to try to protect them by pretending that nothing is wrong. They will sense your anguish. What children need to know now is that death is not a taboo subject in your family. Your willingness to discuss this with them reassures them that "we can talk about anything." Speak openly about what has happened, but don't burden them with more information than they need. Give short, direct answers to their questions. And keep in mind that overheard telephone conversations and whispered exchanges may confuse them.

Give them choices. If they want to see the baby, explain ahead of time what they will see. If they want to be at the memorial gathering, explain what will happen. If they don't want to do these things, give them other ways to feel included such as choosing one of their toys to be sent with the baby for cremation or burial, or making cookies for the memorial gathering.

Children do not see death as permanent, so you may hear them ask later, "When can I play with the baby" or "Is the baby through being dead yet?" Because they can't grasp that a dead body is totally nonfunctioning they may wonder if the baby is cold or hungry. And they don't understand that sooner or later death happens to everyone.

Very young children will be more upset by the disruptions in their family environment and feeling that their needs are not being met. They may react negatively to changes in the home caused by death like interruption of daily routine, such as the constant stream of visitors, their parents' sadness, and the focus of attention away from them.

Let your children know that the baby won't be in their daily life, but that they can still remember the baby. Explain as best you can what caused the baby to die, e.g. the baby's body was too small, his stomach was not big enough, her lungs hadn't learned how to breathe, the baby's body couldn't be fixed, etc.. Explain also that people who are dead cannot see, eat, breathe, play, or feel pain.

Assure the children that nothing they did caused the baby to die. Explain that everyone else in the family is okay and that they are sad, but not sick.

As parents, we don't have to have all the answers. When children ask 'why' it is okay for parents to answer, "We wish we knew. But we don't". Rephrasing their questions and asking for their opinions may help them tell you what they are thinking. Their answers may surprise you.

You may want to take your other children for a walk in your neighborhood and look for examples to help you explain death to your childlike leaves falling from a tree, rosebuds that don't open, a dead bird lying on the ground, an egg that has fallen from its nest.

Let them know that some people are sad on the inside and others will be sad on the outside and will show their sadness by crying. Reassure them when they see you cry that you are crying because you miss the baby, not because of their behavior. Share hugs. Read books that will help them to project their feelings onto the story characters.

Things you can do to remember the baby.

Light a candle for the baby on special days
Celebrate the baby's life no matter how short
Make a memory box or scrapbook
Give the child a gift from the baby
Have your children write a story about the baby.

Plant a tree or a bush
Take a picture of the child with the baby
Draw pictures of the family
Make a clay model of the baby

Finally, take care of yourselves. Accept offers of help. Make sure there are other adults who can be with your children when you are not emotionally available to them. Trust that no one is ever too young to deal with the hard parts of life. It would be nice if we could protect our children from all of this. But we are not trusting their innate wisdom if we deny them the opportunity to share this time with them.
For additional information we invite you to go to www.griefwatch.com.